W9-AVD-221

STATE SHOWDOWN

A Random House book
Published by Random House Australia Pty Ltd
Level 3, 100 Pacific Highway, North Sydney NSW 2060
www.randomhouse.com.au

First published by Random House Australia in 2015

Copyright © Random House Australia 2015

The moral right of the author and the illustrator has been asserted.

All rights reserved. No part of this book may be reproduced or transmitted by any
person or entity, including internet search engines or retailers, in any form or by any
means, electronic or mechanical, including photocopying (except under the statutory
exceptions provisions of the Australian *Copyright Act 1968*), recording, scanning or by
any information storage and retrieval system without the prior written permission of
Random House Australia.

Addresses for companies within the Random House Group can be found at
global.penguinrandomhouse.com

National Library of Australia
Cataloguing-in-Publication Entry

Author: Loughlin, Patrick.
Title: State showdown/Patrick Loughlin, with contributions from Glenn Maxwell;
        illustrated by James Hart.
ISBN: 978 0 85798 611 5 (pbk)
Series: Glenn Maxwell; 3.
Target Audience: For primary school age.
Subjects: Cricket – Australia – Juvenile fiction.
        Cricket players – Australia – Juvenile fiction.
Other Authors/Contributors: Maxwell, Glenn.
        Hart, James, illustrator.
Dewey Number: A823.4

The publisher would like to thank Macquarie Dictionary for use of definitions
in Macquarie Dictionary Online, 2014, Macquarie Dictionary's Publishers,
https://www.macquariedictionary.com.au

Illustrations by James Hart
Image of Glenn Maxwell courtesy of Kookaburra Sport Pty Ltd
Cover design by Christabella Designs
Typeset by Midland Typesetters, Australia
Printed in Australia by Griffin Press, an accredited ISO AS/NZS 14001:2004
Environmental Management System printer

Random House Australia uses papers that are natural, renewable
and recyclable products and made from wood grown in sustainable
forests. The logging and manufacturing processes are expected to
conform to the environmental regulations of the country of origin.

STATE SHOWDOWN

WRITTEN BY
PATRICK LOUGHLIN

ILLUSTRATED BY
JAMES HART

RANDOM HOUSE AUSTRALIA

BIG FISH

WHAP!

The cricket ball whistled through the air, bounced once in the outfield, then leapt happily over the fence for four.

It was the first game of the season and Will Albright was having a blinder. He was already

44 off 17 balls. His run rate was phenomenal for a club match.

The stocky kid from the East Heights club who was steaming in from the northern end had gotten faster since last year but to Will, it seemed like he was moving in slow motion compared to the supersonic speed of the T20 Academy bowlers like Darren 'Killer' McKinnon. In fact, the entire pace of club cricket seemed slow to Will now.

Will cracked another short ball for a whopping six to bring up his half-century. As he watched the shoulders of the East Heights bowler slump, Will almost felt guilty. It was too easy.

'Way to go, Will!' Mr Albright called at the top of his lungs, before throwing in

a whistle for extra encouragement. Will's mum was waving excitedly as well. Even Will's 64-year-old nanna, who had come along especially to watch Will in the first game of the season, was clapping with gusto – in a refined-nanna kind of way.

The Green Park Rangers took to the field in the second innings to defend their impressive total of 147. But by the tenth over, the team's fast bowlers had claimed just two wickets and Will made the captain's call to bring on the spinners.

This season, Will was one of them. The other spinner, Aaron Mooney, was a tidy bowler but he didn't have Will's variation or his Glenn-Maxwell-inspired top-secret carrom ball. While Aaron helped restrain the run rate, it was Will who proved more deadly to the East Heights batsmen.

In his first over, Will delivered a jagging off-spinner that curled back on the batsman and skimmed off the edge of the bat into the waiting hands of the keeper. In his second over, he produced a topspinner that fooled the new East Heights batsman completely and smashed through the leg stump. Two balls later, he unleashed the carrom ball. Will casually stepped up to the popping crease and rolled his arm over, carefully hiding his grip so his ball would be a surprise.

The East Heights batsman didn't have a clue what hit him. First, Will flicked the ball out to the off side and it beat the batsman completely. It even fooled the wicketkeeper, who missed the pick-up, and the ball rolled almost all the way to the fence before being chased down by a fielder. For the next ball, Will flicked the ball to the leg side and the batsman went after it. Unfortunately for the batsman, he was fooled again and the ball slid past the bat and onto his pads. He was given LBW and reluctantly walked away, shaking his head and trying to work out just what it was he had been beaten by. At the end of the over, Will tossed the ball back to Aaron who shrugged. 'You may as well keep it; I can't do that.'

Will waved Aaron's comment away, but inside he was quite pleased. His cricket had come a long way since last season and it was all down to being selected for the academy and making the state team. With his new-found skill, he could almost single-handedly obliterate the opposition!

At the end of the match, Will and the boys celebrated in the change rooms. Will had the best figures for batting and bowling.

'Will, that was one of the most amazing individual performances at this club I've ever witnessed,' said Geoff, the Green Park coach. 'If you keep that up, we'll be in the grand final again this year!'

'Thanks, Geoff,' said Will with a grin. But as he looked around the change room at his teammates, he couldn't help notice that some had turned away.

'I guess joining the academy has really helped you accelerate your skill level, hey?' said Geoff.

'Yeah, I guess. There're so many great players there that you really have to go up a gear,' said Will, but, again, he was distracted when two of his teammates rolled their eyes at each other.

'So now you've come back to club cricket, you're the big fish,' said Geoff.

'Big fish?' said Will, still a little distracted by the eye rolling.

'You're the big fish in the little pond here, Will. You were running rings around those other guys out there today! But don't worry, that's good for us – at least until you go off to play with the state squad,' grinned Geoff. 'Then I'll need some of these other minnows to step up!' he said, pointing his head in the direction of the other players. It was meant to be a joke but no one laughed.

Will decided to play things down a little. 'Well, I guess I'll be back to being a little fish when I go into the state team,' he said, trying to sound suitably modest.

'Hey, don't you let those other state players

intimidate you. You don't have to be the little fish. Just starting thinking big,' advised Geoff.

'Okay, I'll try. Thanks, Geoff,' said Will. He began packing up his gear and looked around the room once more. All the other players looked away, some at the wall, some at their bags, some at nothing at all. Only Geoff kept smiling back at Will.

Well, this is a little awkward, thought Will. *I don't get why they're acting like this. Are they jealous?*

Will had played with most of these boys for the past three years.

Just because I'm in the T20 Academy and I've made the state side doesn't mean I've changed. I'm still the same old Will!

'See ya next week,' said Will. There were a few half-nods and grunts but only one decent

'See ya'. Will shook his head and headed back out into the bright November sunlight, to the car where his dad was waiting for him.

Oh well, who needs them? Next month I'll be playing for Victoria! And maybe Geoff is right. All I need to do is think big. No more negativity; no more doubting myself. From now on, I'll play like I did today: with total confidence. When I get back to the academy, I'm going to be the big fish in the big pond!

MR POSITIVITY

Three weeks later, Will leapt off the green and gold St Kilda Beach tram with his cricket kitbag slung over his shoulder and darted through the gates of the academy training centre like someone had poured some rather hyperactive ants down his pants. He couldn't wait to get to training.

Since the announcement of the Junior Boys' Victorian T20 team, things had been a little slow at the academy. Besides a training clinic in the September holidays, there had been an extended break in training because almost half the state squad was from regional Victoria, which made it difficult to get everyone together. The boys were encouraged to use their training and club matches to stay fit and hone their skills, but now that the national competition was just two weeks away, the whole team was finally coming together for an intense training camp. All the country players would be staying at the academy centre in brand-new overnight accommodation facilities. Will was a little jealous that the city kids couldn't stay, too.

Well, at least he got the last two weeks of school off.

Will hurdled a sprinkler that was *snicker-snacking* its way across the pristine lawn, tore up the steps of the large, white academy building and skidded through the glass sliding doors. He casually flashed his ID card at the man behind the reception desk and dashed to the lifts, feeling almost ready to burst.

As the lift doors began to close, they were halted by a single large fist jamming its way between the silver metal lips. It was Killer.

Will pushed the open-door button and let Darren 'Killer' McKinnon in.

Will nodded hello and Darren grunted back as the lift began ascending.

Suddenly, Will called out, 'Wait! Stop!'

Darren jumped. 'What?'

'You forgot Teddy,' said Will.

Darren squirmed. When Will and Darren had shared a cabin at the T20 Academy Cricket Camp, Will had discovered Darren's secret: he still slept with a little brown teddy bear.

'I don't sleep with Winky anymore,' mumbled Darren.

'Winky?' asked Will, barely able to stifle a chuckle.

'Shut up,' said Darren, but he shook his head and snorted a laugh.

This is going to be fun, thought Will as the lift doors opened. The two boys had grown a little closer since the training camp, and now that they were on the same team Will felt confident enough to poke fun at Killer. A big change from the first time they'd met.

Once inside the indoor training hall, Will and Darren found that a few members of the squad were already there, hitting some practice balls in the nets. Will spotted his friend Shavil Kumar and waved.

'Hey Shavil, ready to take on the rest of Australia?'

Shavil laughed. 'I guess so. What about you?'

'Oh, I'm super-ready. We're gonna slaughter them!'

'Okay,' replied Shavil awkwardly. He wasn't used to seeing Will so gung-ho. 'Aren't you even a tiny bit nervous, though? We're going to be up against the best junior players in the country.'

'Why should we be nervous? We're just as good as anyone else,' said Will, his eyes bright with conviction.

'Did you stop and have a blue slushie on the way here?' asked Shavil. 'You seem a little wired.'

'Well, yes – two, actually. But that's not why I'm excited! This is going to be huge!' shouted Will, a little too loudly. 'If we play well, we could end up in the Australian team. We could be flying to England for the T20 Youth World Cup next year!'

Shavil eyed Will suspiciously. He was clearly hyped up on slushie sugar. 'Well, I guess it's always good to be positive,' he said finally.

'Just call me Mr Positivity,' said Will, bouncing his eyebrows eagerly.

'I'll stick with "Will",' said Shavil.

A few minutes later, Jack Jarrett, the T20 state selector and coach, entered the hall, followed by some of the players from the Victorian Bushrangers. Glenn Maxwell was one of them and there were a lot of sudden gasps and excited chatter from the boys in the squad when they noticed Glenn and the players strolling into the training room.

Jack was carrying a large cardboard box and had a mysterious grin on his face that suggested something special was about to happen.

'Welcome back to the academy, boys,' said Jack as the boys began crowding around. 'You're about to take on your toughest test yet: the T20 National Youth Shield.' He looked around at the group of boys. 'Repre-senting your state is a privilege, one that you have earned after a lot of hard work. That's why I've asked some of our state's best players from the Victorian Bushrangers to present you with your state caps.'

Will couldn't believe that he was this close to the Bushrangers. He crossed his fingers and hoped that it would be his cricketing hero, Glenn Maxwell, who would present him with his cap.

'Hey, where's Brock?' whispered Will to Shavil as they waited quietly. Brock had been at T20 Youth Academy earlier in the year. If he was honest with himself, Will had been a bit jealous of Brock – of how good a batsman he was . . . of how much his friend Zoe had liked him . . . Will hadn't really been looking forward to seeing Brock again.

'Didn't you hear? His dad had to go back to Perth for work so the whole family moved again.'

'Oh,' said Will. 'That sucks.'

He felt bad for Brock but couldn't help wondering about the opener position that was now vacant. Although he'd gotten used to the idea of being an all-rounder now that his spin bowling was getting stronger, he still sometimes fantasised about being a star batsman.

'– which brings us to Will Albright, right-arm off-spinner and number-six batsman,' announced Jack proudly.

I guess that answers that question, thought Will. *Whoever's taking the opening position, it's not me.*

Will looked up to see the familiar face of Glenn Maxwell and his moment of disappointment quickly disappeared. Will almost had to pinch himself. Glenn Maxwell was going to present him with his Victorian cap!

'Well done, Will,' said Glenn handing Will his cap and shaking his hand.

'Thanks, Maxi. I'm not sure I would have got here without your help,' said Will.

'No worries, Will, anytime. Have a great tournament, okay? Give it to those other states!'

As Jack moved on to the next player, Will looked down at the cap in his hand and ran his fingers over the lettering of the emblem.

I can't wait to show everyone I'm up to the challenge!

Once all the boys had their caps, Jack addressed the group again.

'I hope you're as excited as I am to have the Bushrangers here. They'll be sticking around for a while to offer some advice during training. But that's not all . . . I have some special news. I just found out today that the final of the National Youth Shield will be played before the Melbourne Stars' first game of the T20 Big Bash League against the Sydney Sixers at the MCG!'

The squad erupted into cheers.

'Let's not get ahead of ourselves just yet,' said Jack. 'Tomorrow we'll find out the draw and which group we're in. No matter who we're up against, we're going to have to play well to get through to the finals.'

A few of the boys nodded and there was a brief silence as they took in Jack's words.

'Well, what are you waiting for?' said Jack, breaking the reverie. 'Let's get training!'

LUCK OF THE DRAW

Will watched the wisps of clouds float across the blue sky above him and realised one irrefutable fact: summer rules.

The first great thing about summer was daylight saving. It was almost 6 pm but the sun had only just begun to sink behind the city skyline. Will loved the feeling of getting home from training in the daylight rather than in complete darkness. The second great thing was the weather. Finally they were getting some relief from Melbourne's freezing winter and chilly spring. But by far the best thing about summer was that it was cricket season.

After a gruelling two-hour long training session, Will had stopped for a rest on the concrete steps of the academy centre. He'd just finished training with Glenn Maxwell, bowling a few deliveries to his hero and facing Maxi's own off-spin deliveries. As he sat there, he noticed that the junior girls' team was still out on the oval doing some catching drills. There was a round of cheers from the oval. It sounded like the girls were finished. Will took a swig of water and watched as the girls began packing up their gear.

I need to time this just right, thought Will. He grabbed his cricket kitbag and headed off down the steps, dawdling just a little as he got to the driveway that led to the car park. As each of the girls walked past him, Will kept an eye out for Zoe, the feisty, curly haired team captain that Will had grown fond of since they'd first met at the T20 camp. He'd been hoping to bump into her. When there was no one left to walk past him, he got worried.

Where is Zoe?

Will found out the answer to his question the next day at the tournament draw when he saw Zoe standing next to her uncle, coach Jack Jarrett, with her arm in a sling.

Will made his way through the crowd of players, coaching staff and family that was getting bigger and bigger as more of the state teams arrived at the academy centre, over to where Jack and Zoe were standing.

'What happened?' gasped Will when he had finally gotten through the throng of people.

'I fractured my wrist diving for a catch at training,' said Zoe, her face dark with disappointment.

But they had only been at training for one day! 'Yesterday?' Will asked.

Zoe nodded. 'It was my own fault. I was showing off. I just launched myself at the ball without thinking and came straight down on my wrist.'

'So how are you going to play?' Will realised it was a stupid question as soon as it left his mouth.

'I can't,' said Zoe bitterly.

Will smiled nervously at Zoe but he couldn't think of a single thing to say. Usually they talked about cricket but Will figured it would be the last thing that Zoe would want to think about right now.

'Okay, well I better get this show on the road,' said Jack, interrupting Will's thoughts.

There was a squeal of feedback from the

PA, followed by the sound of Jack blowing into the microphone.

'Testing . . . Thanks for coming, everyone. It's great that you're all going to have the chance to enjoy our new facilities. We're going to get the draw underway now,' crackled Jack's voice through the mic. 'Can I get all the team captains to come up please?'

Will watched as a number of players made their way up the stairs to the makeshift stage that had been set up outside the entrance. Soon there were a lot of players on the stage. There was a captain for each state and territory for the under 14s and 16s for both the girls' and boys' teams, including his own team captain, Mike Reynolds. Zoe was not one of them.

Will looked over at Zoe. Her face was blank.

If it were me, I'd be crushed, thought Will.

'And now I'd like to call on the president of the Victorian T20 Youth Academy, Bob Cruickshank, to announce the draw,' said Jack. A distinguished-looking gentleman came to the podium and accepted an envelope from Jack. The crowd went silent as he opened it and began reading out the groups of teams in a rough, quavering voice.

'Well boys, it's Group A for us. It isn't the group of death but it's pretty close,' said Jack at the team debrief after the draw. 'I'm confident we can beat the ACT. But New South Wales and Tasmania? We're going to have to work hard to win against those two teams. Remember: only the top two teams from each group go through to the semifinals.'

Group B was made up of Western Australia, South Australia, Queensland and the Northern Territory. Will thought that had they been in Group B the competition wouldn't have been any easier, especially considering that Western Australia would have Brock opening for them.

As the rest of the squad left, Jack called Will over for a chat.

'Will, given that we're up against the ACT first and we want to get off to a good start, I was thinking that I might promote you up the order, what do you think?'

Will was a little surprised. Perhaps Jack had more faith in his batting than he'd thought.

'Whatever you need me to do, Jack.'

'Good, Will, that's what I want to hear.'

Will couldn't help grinning. Maybe his positive thinking was already paying off. Victoria needed to win the shield and he was determined to play a starring role.

'I won't let you down.'

SKY HIGH

The coin twirled through the air and landed on the pitch of the academy oval with a soft plonk.

'Heads,' said the umpire.

The ACT captain had called tails so Mike, the Victorian team captain, got first choice. 'We'll bat first,' said Mike.

A few minutes later, Riley Brennan — the replacement opener for Brock — and Shavil walked out to the crease for Victoria's first shield match.

'We've got a quality team and if we execute the game plan well, we should win this. But let's not underestimate our opposition,' Jack had said before the game.

They turned out to be wise words. On the second ball of the first over, Riley played a hook shot. The ball nicked the edge of the bat, popped up two metres in the air and landed in the waiting gloves of the keeper.

'That's not a good start,' huffed Jack, under his breath. He turned to Will. 'All right. You're up. Show them we mean business.'

Will walked out to the middle, eyeing the small crowd of spectators that had turned out to watch the game. They were mostly the families and friends of the players but there were a few St Kilda locals who had come down to watch the show.

All right, Will, stay cool. Get used to the conditions first before you cut loose, Will told himself.

But when the ACT bowler sent down his first ball to Will – a lazy, medium pacer outside off stump – Will couldn't resist.

KEEERRRAAACK!

The bowler, the umpire and all the fielders craned their necks as a little red comet passed over their heads and vanished behind the grandstand.

The umpire raised his hands and signalled six and the spectators erupted in applause.

Will suddenly felt a whole lot taller.

So much for getting used to the conditions. I'm ready to let rip!

Will slashed the next ball through covers for four. Another cheer went up from the crowd and Will smiled. *I could get used to this.*

After the last ball of the over – a full delivery that Will blocked safely away – he met Shavil in the middle. Shavil punched Will's glove.

'Ouch!' said Shavil, shaking his glove in mock pain. 'You're on fire!'

It took Will by surprise, but then he grinned.

'So, what's the plan?' asked Shavil. He asked Will this every time they batted

together and Will usually gave the same response. Today was no exception, only today he said it without a single doubt in his mind.

'Stay calm, hit big, don't get out,' said Will.

'Good call,' said Shavil.

Shavil took the crease at the striker's end and began in his trademark careful style. He played the first ball with a firm forward stroke, sending the ball rolling along the ground and taking a quick single. Will took up the strike and was less cautious in his approach. The bowler ran in and fired a little red rocket that was dead on target for the wicket but Will took two quick steps down the pitch and effortlessly launched the ball back over the bowler's head.

The umpire signalled six again. Will skipped to 18 off four balls but he was just warming up. The next three balls were like watching instant replay: each time, the ball hit the pitch just outside off stump and Will dropped to his knee and swept the ball to the fence for four.

CRACK! Four.

SMASH! Four.

THUMP! Four.

The people in the crowd, who had risen to their feet and cheered each boundary, were starting to look a little dizzy from hopping up and down.

On the last ball of the over, just to be different, the bowler tried a bouncer. Will hooked it for six and after that, most of the crowd remained standing.

They weren't disappointed. On the first ball of the third over, Shavil took another careful single and Will returned to the striker's end and continued the onslaught.

The small collection of ACT supporters put their heads in their hands and wished that it would end soon.

When Victoria took to the field for the second innings, they were already easily on top with a commanding total of five for 196. The ACT supporters cautiously opened their eyes to see how their batters would fare but had to close them rather quickly as Darren was unleashed onto the unsuspecting ACT openers. He snatched two scalps with two blistering deliveries. After the first over, ACT were two for nought. Six overs in and ACT had recovered a little, at four for 54. That's when Mike handed the ball to Will.

'Let's keep the pressure on,' said Mike. Will nodded and headed to the non-striker's end. He looked at the field, frowned and then called Mike over.

'I don't think we need a second slip in,' said Will.

Mike screwed up his face in confusion. 'What? Of course we do. I want an attacking field: we're trying to apply pressure.'

'I've been watching this guy and he's not going after much on the off side. I think I can get him with someone at short mid-wicket,' said Will.

'Well, I don't,' said Mike.

There was an awkward pause.

'Okay,' said Will.

He walked back to the crease and began his over. He started with his stock off-break but didn't get enough spin or flight on it and the batter slotted it through the on side field for two runs. Next, Will tried a topspinner to entice the batsman to play at it and get an outside edge. But, despite their desperate need for runs, the ACT batsman let it go. Will decided to go back to the off-break, trying a shorter length, and the batsman slashed at it, popping the ball up in the air. Will ran in but he couldn't get to it and the ball fell to the ground safely in the gap.

This is useless, thought Will.

He looked over to Mike at first slip and threw his hands up in the air. Mike glared and shook his head.

Fine. If he won't change the field, I will.

Will signalled to Riley, who was out in the deep at mid-wicket, to move in.

Riley looked nervously over at Mike.

'Get on with it!' called someone from the crowd.

Riley shrugged and moved up to short mid-wicket.

Will didn't look back at Mike. If he had, he would have seen that Mike's face was aghast with disbelief. Instead, Will concentrated on which delivery to bowl. He decided to go with the straight-arm ball he'd been practising. It would look just like the off-break but the straighter line might make the batsman play at it.

Will trotted into the pitch and unleashed the arm ball with gusto. The batsman swiped at the ball and miscued it. It flew straight to Riley at mid-wicket, who couldn't believe his luck. He caught the ball as clean as a whistle and threw it up into the air in celebration. The team ran in and showered Riley with high fives. Then they attacked Will.

Everyone except for Mike.

MR EGOTISTICAL

'Why can't people just accept advice? Why do they have to be so stubborn?' demanded Will.

Zoe, who was trying to watch the Victorian girls' game against South Australia, looked over at Will curiously. 'Who are you talking about now?' she asked only half-interested. Will had been rabbiting on for ages.

'Zoe, haven't you been listening at all? Mike, that's who!' said Will. 'All I did was make one little fielding change, then when we get off the field he starts yelling at me!'

'Wait, you made a fielding change without your captain's permission?' She was clearly unimpressed.

'But . . . but I got the wicket! I took three wickets! We won the game! He should be happy,' argued Will.

'But Will, he's the captain, not you. It's not your call. I wouldn't want someone going against my fielding positions.'

There was a long silence. Will had been on a high after the win, until his run-in with

Mike. Then he'd been angry. Now he was confused. He'd thought Zoe would be on his side. Couldn't she see he was just trying to win his team the game? How was it his fault that Mike's fielding positions weren't good enough?

'Come on girls, get active out there!' called Zoe. Will looked at the field. It wasn't good news for Zoe's team. They were yet to take a wicket; their bowling was being torn apart by the South Australian girls, yet here was Zoe, arm in sling, screaming support for her teammates while Will was whining about his own. At least he could still play.

'How can you sit here and watch? Doesn't it just make you angry you're not out there?' asked Will.

'It's better than staying at home, feeling sorry for myself,' said Zoe. 'I might not be out there playing, but I'm still part of the team. It's not all about me.'

There was another awkward silence as Will sat and thought about Zoe's words.

It's not all about me.

Was she trying to tell him he was being self-centred or did it just feel that way? Maybe he had overstepped the mark a little. Mike *was* captain after all.

'Sorry, Zoe. You're right, I shouldn't complain. And I really wish you could be out there.'

Zoe turned and looked at him. She smiled, but her eyes were glistening just a little. They sparkled in the sunlight and Will thought for just a moment . . .

She's beautiful.

Then she punched him in the arm. 'Jerk!' she said and laughed.

'Ow!' said Will. He rubbed his arm and laughed as well, puzzled.

⚡

'Come on, get on that ball!' yelled Dan Brocklehurst, their fielding coach and fitness trainer.

Will rushed in, stopped the hard-hit ball with his forearm, then scooped it up and fired it back at Dan.

It was training day and Will was keen to impress.

'Good work, Will,' said Dan.

'Thanks,' said Will nonchalantly, 'but maybe we should work on our flat catching – we put down a few chances in that game against the ACT.'

The rest of the team went quiet. Dan was a little annoyed but he was too nice to really show it.

'Um, sure, we might look at that later in the week,' said Dan. His teammates exchanged looks, but Will didn't notice.

Later in the practice nets, Will forgot to put on his helmet when he took up the bat against Darren.

'Aren't you forgetting something?' asked Darren, pointing to his head. He was insulted that Will would dare enter the net and face him without his head protected.

Will made a face. 'Oops. Although, the way I'm playing, I probably don't need a helmet,' joked Will.

'Maybe your head won't fit it anyway,' muttered Darren as Will went off to find his helmet.

Even Shavil was taken aback by Will's over-inflated 'confidence'. When it was Shavil's turn to face Darren in the nets, Will decided to give him a little advice about his stance.

'Step into him, Shavil. Disrupt his length.'

Shavil turned, his eyes flaring in disbelief.

'What?' protested Will. 'I'm just being Mr Positivity, remember?'

'You mean, Mr Egotistical,' said Shavil. 'Since when were you the batting coach?'

'I'm just trying to help!' said Will.

'I think I know what I'm doing,' said Shavil.

It didn't help when Darren bowled Shavil on the next ball. As Shavil retrieved the ball, Will could feel three words travelling from his throat to his mouth. They rolled off the end of his tongue before he could stop them, even though his head knew they were the worst words he could say right now.

'Told you so.'

Shavil's face fell and all at once Will felt terrible. Shavil shook his head, folded his bat under his arm and left the net without another word.

'Well, I did,' said Will weakly as Shavil walked away.

'What's your problem?' asked Darren. Will realised that things must have gotten bad if Darren was accusing him of being mean.

For the rest of training, Will kept his mouth shut but it didn't stop his teammates shooting dark looks in his direction. Everyone seemed to be annoyed at him but Will still didn't understand what all the fuss was about.

Can't they see I'm just trying to help the team?

FISH OUT OF WATER

Later that night as Will lay in bed staring up at his Glenn Maxwell poster, he thought back to the practice session. He still didn't get why his teammates were so upset with him – and his teammates clearly didn't get why he was frustrated with them.

'What would you do, Maxi?' Will asked the larger-than-life poster of Glenn Maxwell. It was an image of Maxi playing another amazing shot for the Victorian Bushrangers. Will brightened. Maxi's answer to his question was right here in front of him, in Glenn Maxwell's frozen moment of glory.

I need to let my playing do the talking instead of my mouth!

He watched Glenn Maxwell's face morph into his own.

I'll show them all what I can do. I'll go out there and play the game of my life, thought Will. *I'm not a little fish; I'm a whale!*

※

Will was standing at the crease out in the middle of the MCG. It was the final of the T20 National Youth Shield. They were playing New South Wales and needed just four runs to win.

'Come on Will, show 'em what you can do!' shouted Shavil from the non-striker's end.

Will nodded and resumed strike as the bowler galloped in. The ball was rocketing towards him. Except somehow the ball looked bigger than it was supposed to. And it kept getting bigger.

Will realised the ball wasn't getting bigger. He was shrinking. He got smaller and smaller till he was the size of a goldfish and the ball looked as big as a boulder.

In a flash the ball was on him. It bounced off the pitch and collected him on the way.

Will held on as the ball burst through the stumps.

'AAARGH!'

The ball thudded to the ground with Will still on it and then it rolled over and over, battering him into the ground as it went. Finally, he fell off and lay in the grass panting in pain until a large head loomed over him, blocking out the sun.

It was the giant face of the umpire.

'You're OUT!' the umpire boomed.

Will couldn't breathe. He looked down and saw that his hands were no longer hands, they were fins. His legs were no longer legs, they had merged into a long orange tail.

I am a little fish, thought Will miserably. *And I'm out . . . and out of water. I need water.*

Will flailed about on the ground, flapping his fins and swishing his tail helplessly from side to side. 'Help!' he screamed. 'Someone help me!'

But no sound came out of his little goldfish mouth.

'Will what are you doing on the floor?'

Will opened his eyes and saw his mother standing over him. It was morning and he was lying on the carpet, tangled up in his doona.

Will remembered: today was the second group game, this one against New South Wales.

Well, joked Will as he untangled himself from his doona, *no matter what happens in*

the game, at least I won't get out and turn into
a fish.

Unfortunately, Will was only half-right.

Will stared at the umpire, watching as he
slowly raised a finger into the air.

Will was out.

The New South Wales team jumped up
and down in celebration. They had a lot to
celebrate: after winning the toss they had
dismissed both openers for just 19 runs. Now
they had dismissed Will.

Will stood there in total disbelief.

When he'd arrived at the crease just five
minutes ago, he'd been feeling confident.

Despite watching both Shavil and Riley go cheaply (Riley to a brilliant yorker that smashed through the stumps and Shavil to a rather dubious LBW call), Will still walked out to the middle of the ground with one thing on his mind: proving that he was better than anyone else out there.

He did all right in the first over. He managed to pull a jagging off-cutter to the fence for four and then grab three runs from a nicely angled deflection off a ball drifting outside leg stump. But when Will faced up for his second over, he decided before the ball had even left the bowler's hand that he was going to belt it back over the bowler's head. What Will didn't realise was that the bowler saw him advancing down the pitch and decided to switch up the pace. Will miscued the ball completely and it struck his front pad straight in front of middle stump. There was nothing dubious about it. He was plumb.

He stood there for a long moment in shock before one of the New South Wales fielders gave Will a wave. 'Come on mate, take a walk.'

Will walked away from the pitch cursing himself.

He cursed himself even more when the second innings began and Victoria had to defend a paltry 117. It was time to make amends for his poor batting performance.

'Mike, you have to put me on, I can get these guys out,' pleaded Will.

'Not yet, Will, let the fast bowlers have a go. There's no turn on this pitch, anyway – what makes you think you can take a wicket?'

'I took three last game, don't you remember? If you set the right field I –'

But Mike wasn't interested in hearing another word.

'Will, *I'm* captain, *I'll* put you on when *I* think we need you,' barked Mike. 'And don't ask me again, or I'll find someone else to bowl.'

But six overs into the innings, after watching his four fast bowlers – including Darren – get belted all around the ground, Mike had changed his mind.

He called Will over. 'All right, you're up. Where do you want the field?'

Will smiled, happy to be proven right. He gave Mike fielding instructions, then he headed to the northern end of the pitch.

Okay, let's start with a nice offie, nothing fancy, he told himself.

But his off-break was a little off target and devoid of flight. The New South Wales captain and opener, whose name on the scoreboard read T Gregg, smashed it to the boundary fence with one mighty sweep.

Okay, not a good start. Stay calm, Will. It's just the first ball.

On the second ball, Will decided to send down the topspinner but the result was much the same: T Gregg employed the sweep shot again and this time the ball made it over the fence and was caught by a rather large lady in the crowd.

Who does he think he is, Glenn Maxwell?
wondered Will.

Will looked over at Mike. He did not look happy.

Okay, time to pull out the big guns. Let's see how he handles the carrom ball.

Will had developed his version of the carrom ball after Maxi had suggested he work on his spin bowling. He'd been working hard on perfecting it and he knew if he got it right, it could fool any batsman.

But T Gregg, the New South Wales opener, obviously was not just any batsman. He was good. Really good. And poor Will could only stand and watch as his carrom ball delivery – the one he had worked so hard on – disappeared into the blue sky.

Another six. And it didn't end there. Every ball that Will bowled in his first over went to the boundary. He was 30 off six. Great figures for a batsman, terrible for a bowler.

After an equally poor second over, Mike removed Will from the attack. Not that it made much difference. New South Wales needed just 12 runs to win.

It was all over in a matter of minutes and when New South Wales scored the winning runs, Will watched on powerlessly. He felt as helpless as a fish out of water, but this time it was no dream.

HUMBLE PIE

Will wearily climbed the stairs of the academy centre. As he passed through the glass entrance door, he winced at the big bold letters of the academy motto staring down at him: Team above self. Heart above all else.

The game against New South Wales was all he'd thought about for the past two days. On the night of the match he'd gone to bed thinking about it, the next day he had woken up thinking about it and, of course, he had thought about it all that day. That was Wednesday and Thursday. Today was Friday, and Will was dreading training.

After the game against New South Wales, the mood in the change rooms had been terrible. It had been deathly quiet. No one had said a word. Except for Jack, who had spoken in a low, soft tone, as if he were talking at a funeral.

'Boys, we can take a few things away from losing the game. New South Wales played very well. Sometimes, you get outplayed and there's nothing you can do. We were outgunned today, simple as that. Now we have to move on . . .'

Even though most of his teammates had their heads down at the time, Will was sure he could feel them all glaring at him, blaming him for the team's loss.

Now he was dragging his feet into training. He knew he would have to face similar glaring and silent blame. He also knew that he'd have to eat a large plate of humble pie, as his dad would say.

'Oi! Will!'

He turned to see the buoyant smiling face of Shavil.

At least Shavil wasn't ignoring him.

'Fancy a hit?' he asked.

'Sure,' said Will.

'You bowl first,' said Shavil, tossing Will a ball. 'Give us that carrom ball; I want to know how good it is,' said Shavil.

Will smiled for the first time that day, but when he came in and delivered the ball, flicking it out to the right, it skidded off the edge of the green synthetic pitch and crashed into the back of the net.

'What was that?' asked a puzzled Shavil.

Will shrugged. He didn't know. He'd practised that ball over and over. Sure, he didn't always get it right – but he didn't usually get it that wrong.

When he stepped up and attempted the carrom ball a second time . . .

CRASH!

. . . he missed the pitch completely.

What the heck?

'Hello, Will, I'm over here?' joked Shavil with a cute little wave.

'I just . . .' Will looked down at his fingers, expecting to see some of them missing. 'I need to warm up my fingers first,' said Will.

'Fine, I'll bowl first, then,' announced Shavil, trotting down the pitch and swapping bat for ball. 'It will give me a chance to test out my own mystery ball. I call it . . . The Mongoose.' His eyes lit up and he bounced his eyebrows up and down excitedly, making Will laugh a little.

'Whatever,' said Will, grabbing his trusty Kookaburra from his bag. He took up the crease and stared back down the lane at Shavil.

But when Shavil tossed down the ball and Will took a swing, there was a large hollow *clank* on the metal practice stumps.

He'd been clean-bowled by Shavil.

THE LONG WALK BACK

'I wouldn't worry about it,' said Shavil, after training finished and they were heading out the exit gate of the academy. 'Everyone has off days. I bet even Maxi does.'

'But I've been off all week,' said Will, thinking of his poor performance against New South Wales.

'What if I'm the same against Tasmania tomorrow?'

'Will, relax. You worry too much,' said Shavil. 'You're probably just tired. A good night's sleep and you'll be fine,' he added helpfully.

But Will did not sleep well that night and when he got to the academy the next day for the final group game, he felt far from fine.

Tasmania won the toss but elected to bowl. Shavil and Riley both started well. When Shavil nicked a well-angled ball straight to first slip, Victoria was already on 76 runs off nine overs so Will shouldn't have been feeling too much pressure when he went on to replace him. But as he walked out to the middle, his stomach began growling like a dog at an unexpected knock at the door.

'Good luck,' said Shavil as they passed each other in the outfield. 'Look out for that left-hander, he's tough to get away.'

Will nodded and tried to stay positive, but right from the first ball he knew that something was wrong. His rhythm was gone; he couldn't get his feet and arms working together.

The bowler that Shavil had warned him about – a long-legged left-hander – delivered six razor-sharp balls in a row and Will failed to connect his bat to a single one. The final ball hit his glove so hard he dropped his bat. Luckily the ball fell short of the keeper.

'You're out already, you just don't know it,' said the Tasmanian wicketkeeper. Then he yelled loudly to the rest of his teammates. 'Come on, we've got this one, boys!'

I can't get out. Just stick at it. Runs will come, Will told himself.

But the next over was more of the same from the Tasmanian bowlers. It was a different bowler but with the same result: Will just couldn't score. The few shots he did manage to play went straight to fielders. Six dot balls was bad enough in T20, but after ten, even Riley at the non-striker's end was getting worried. When yet another ball skated by Will, Riley raised his arms in the air as if to ask, 'What's wrong?'

Will shrugged, but having his batting partner hurry him up didn't inspire him with confidence. Will was even less focused on the next delivery, a well-pitched thumper that darted up off the pitch and struck Will hard in the ribs. He had to walk away from the crease and take a breath.

On the last ball, though, he got lucky. He was so distracted by the pain echoing through his body that he didn't think, and somehow he managed to push it away to mid-off for a quick single.

Finally he was off the mark – but by scoring his first run off the last ball of the over, he had unwittingly retained the strike and now had to face the long-legged leftie again. After three more dot balls, Will was crumbling under the pressure. When he struck the fourth ball cleanly and it went straight to a fielder at long-on who quickly cut off the single, Will couldn't help hanging his head in despair.

'It's Twenty20. You're supposed to score, remember?' taunted the wickie in Will's ear.

Will couldn't stand it any longer.

All right. Enough mucking about, just go for it!

On the last ball of the over, Will charged down the pitch with the intention of finding the boundary at any cost. Instead, he lifted the ball straight up into the air and found the fieldsman at mid-off.

'Nice work, mate,' shot the wicketkeeper. 'Come back any time.'

Will was out for just one off 18. A golden duck would have been less shameful. The walk back to the pavilion was the longest in Will's life.

BATTLE SCARS

'Tough out there today?' asked Jack when Will got back to the Victorian players' area.

Will nodded. He looked down at the dried blood around his thumbnail and the purple patch of bruise spread across his knuckles from the ball that had hit his glove. His ribs were still stinging too. But the worst sting of all was knowing that this was probably his poorest batting performance ever.

It was lucky that Mike and Darren managed to put a good seventh-wicket partnership together and build a respectable total. Victoria had reached 124 by the twentieth over, but they would have to bowl and field out of their skin to defend it.

'Let's get out there and win this thing!' said Jack, a huge grin splashed across his face.

At least someone's still positive, thought Will. He wasn't looking forward to the next hour one bit.

Will stood at square leg. He felt the breeze whipping across the academy oval and the midday sun streaming through some fast-moving clouds above. Then he noticed Shavil standing over at mid-wicket, making silly faces at him. Will made one back.

And that was all it took. One silly face for him to realise that maybe things weren't so bleak. Maybe he was just having a bad day. Then he remembered what Zoe had said: the team was more than just him. Maybe there was a glimmer of hope yet.

When Darren took two quick wickets, Will's glimmer of hope became a supernova. Victoria was still in the game.

Will kept his head down and focused on fielding well. He didn't want to make any mistakes or let the team down again. Soon Mike was signalling him.

'Start warming up,' he said.

'You still want me to bowl? After last time?' asked Will.

'Of course, we need your spin,' said Mike. 'As long as the field is up to your satisfaction, of course.'

Will looked around at the field placing and nodded. 'Looks okay . . . Oh, you're being sarcastic, huh?'

Mike gave Will a 'no kidding' look. 'Just take some wickets, Will, and don't give away any runs — it's not that hard.'

Will hoped Mike was right.

After he warmed up a little, Will took up the ball and stood at the northern end of the pitch, contemplating his first ball. *Nothing fancy, just a regulation off-break.*

He probably should have tried something a little more fancy as the Tasmanian batsman simply hoicked the ball over the fence for six.

Will tried to swallow down the large lump of embarrassment that had formed in his throat. He looked over at Mike, who was rubbing his eyes with his hands, probably trying to remove the image of Will's first ball from his eyes.

Not a good start.

Will delivered his second ball, another off-break but with more pace. It landed in almost the same spot, right at the batsman's feet, and he pounded it to the fence for four.

AAARGH! Will screamed inside.

When the fielder finally retrieved the ball and threw it to Will, he took it in one hand, raised it to his eye and nodded. He had no idea what his plan was but he didn't want the batsman to know. He didn't want Mike and the rest of the team to know, either.

So make a plan! he told himself.

Will looked at the ball again and it came to him, simple and clear.

Spin the ball.

It sounded obvious, but when Will thought about it he realised that was exactly where he had been going wrong. He needed to get the ball turning through the air and hope that it hit the pitch and turned some more.

He really just had to rip it.

So on his third ball he did exactly that. He threw all his power into his right wrist and slammed his foot down on the crease as he let the ball rip from his fingers.

It wasn't the most accurate ball but it beat the bat.

Now the topspinner. Rip it!

He gave it everything. He tried to imagine every little ounce of energy – every single atom coursing inside his body – suddenly being expelled through his hand.

He bowled the topspinner. It didn't just beat the bat, it bounced up off the pitch and took out leg stump.

Will had his wicket. And it had only taken four balls.

The team rushed in to congratulate him.

'Nice one, Will!' said Mike, almost throttling Will's neck in celebration. 'You had me worried there for a second.'

'Me too,' said Will, stunned.

In his second over, Will took another wicket, then another in his fourth. After that, Killer came back on and chipped in with two more quick wickets.

Despite their modest total, Victoria bowled out Tasmania and won the match with 17 balls to spare.

And although Will couldn't help but be happy that his team was through to the semi-final, he wasn't happy with himself. Sure, he'd taken some wickets, but there was still the issue of his dismal batting. He needed to fix it. But how?

MAXI TO THE RESCUE

Will entered the practice room with his cricket kitbag on his shoulder and fumbled for the light panel on the wall. He switched on the lights and the large overhead fluorescents flickered to life. Will stared for a moment at the empty practice nets and the big empty space. Where normally there would be a heap of boys running and throwing, bowling and batting, today it was just him. He had decided to come in two hours before training to try to get his batting action under control before the semifinal.

He moved the bowling machine to the top of the first lane, filled the feeder with the specially designed, dimpled plastic balls, and set the machine to random delivery mode. Then he grabbed the remote, headed to the back of the lane and pressed the release button.

Beep.

A ball flew from the machine. Will went after it . . . and missed.

Beep.

Out flew another. This time, Will got his bat to it but it nicked the edge and went behind him.

Will faced ball after ball from the machine, some fast, some slow, some medium-paced, some spin. But even with no match pressure and no one else around, he just couldn't get his rhythm back.

After half an hour of swinging away at all types of deliveries, Will was about to pack it in when he was startled by a loud accusing voice.

'What the heck do you think you're up to?'

Will jumped and turned to find a familiar, twinkling smile beaming away at him.

'Gotcha,' said Zoe, impressed with herself. 'Why are you here this early, anyway?'

Will hesitated. He didn't want to talk about his crisis of confidence with Zoe but then he figured she'd probably already heard all about it.

'Trying to improve my batting. You?'

'Came to help my uncle with his mountains of paperwork . . . So, batting issues, huh?' Zoe asked.

Will shrugged. 'I think I've forgotten how to bat.' He was only half-joking.

'Don't worry, I'll just get Maxi up here. He'll remind you,' said Zoe with a devious smile.

Zoe took out her phone and began tapping away with her good hand.

'What are you doing?'

'Shhh,' she said, dismissing Will's question. 'Done.'

'No way, you did not just text Maxi. How do you even have his number?' asked a bemused Will.

'My uncle, of course.'

Suddenly, Zoe's phone beeped. 'He's on his way,' she said.

'What? Really?' asked Will. But Zoe didn't have a chance to reply. The lift door opened and in walked Glenn with his phone in his hand and a large smile on his face.

Will's mouth dropped.

'Hey, Will,' said Glenn. 'I got a text. "Batting emergency at the academy – come ASAP."'

Zoe couldn't help herself. She burst into a fit of hysterical laughter while Will just shook his head. 'You set me up,' said Will.

'Well, yeah,' admitted Zoe, once her laughing fit had subsided. 'Glenn had just arrived and when I saw you were the only one signed in I thought it might be a good time for a batting intervention.'

'What do you mean?' asked Will defensively.

'Will, I saw you out there against Tasmania. It wasn't pretty.'

'At least I'm able to play,' said Will before he could stop himself.

'So I can't be out there, playing for my team. But at least I'm supporting them, which is more than I can say for you. I don't know what's got into you, Will. You're blowing it!'

There was an awkward moment of silence. Will knew Zoe was right but for some reason he was finding it hard to admit it.

'Um, I think what Zoe means is that we need to get you back in form for the semi-final,' Glenn said politely. 'Congrats on making it, by the way.'

'Thanks, Maxi', said Will. He tried to put his pride aside. 'I guess I could use a hand. I don't know what the problem is.' Actually, Will did know. 'I was trying to be the big fish, then I had a dream I was a fish —'

'You had a dream you were a fish?' interrupted Zoe.

'Never mind that,' said Will sharply. 'I just mean, I was trying hard to think positive and to be confident and to play well — but now I just can't seem to find my rhythm,' explained Will.

'Hmm. The Big Fish, huh?' said Glenn dubiously. 'Sounds a bit like the nickname I got saddled with: The Big Show. Sometimes if you concentrate only on trying to do big things, you end up forgetting the small stuff that's really important.'

'So I shouldn't think positive?' asked Will, a little confused.

'Will, I suggest you don't think at all. Just go out there and play your shots. Trust your instincts and the runs will come,' said Glenn. 'Let's give the bowling machine a go again and this time . . .'

'Don't think?' asked Will.

'Exactly,' said Glenn. 'KISS.'

'I don't get it,' said Will.

'Keep it simple, —'

'– stupid!' Zoe finished, looking a bit too hard at Will.

'Oh,' said Will.

'Just watch that ball and keep swinging,' said Glenn.

Will went back to the crease and tried not to think.

Beep.

The ball flew at him and then straight past him.

'Now, you're trying not to think aren't you?' asked Glenn.

'Um . . . yep. I guess.'

'Just watch the ball and play the shot, Will,' said Glenn.

Will locked his eyes on the two wheels of the bowling machine, waiting for the ball's release.

Beep.

The ball flew at Will.

Will smashed it back down the lane.

'That's it!' said Glenn.

Beep.

Smack! Will whacked another one, straight off the middle of the bat.

Beep.

Will smashed another. And another. And as he sized up each ball and dispatched it cleanly the way it came, there was just one thought running through the back of his brain.

Maybe I can do this!

BATTING UP A STORM

On the afternoon of the semifinal, the boys sat and watched the girls' team take on Queensland. The Victorian girls put up a good fight but weren't strong enough to chase down a large Queenslander total. Will saw how disappointed Zoe was and felt that it was time to swallow his pride and make up.

'Hey, Zoe.'

Zoe gave a little smile but didn't say anything.

'Sorry about the game . . . I'm probably not meant to say this, but I bet you guys would have won if you could have played.' Will gave a tentative smile.

'Thanks, Will,' said Zoe, a little brighter this time.

'And thanks for yesterday with Maxi, it was just what I needed,' added Will.

Zoe nodded. 'I know. And I didn't mean to call you stupid.'

'That's okay. I think I was a bit stupid for a while there,' said Will, and they both laughed. Will's heart felt a little lighter – until he noticed an ominous fleet of black clouds building in the west.

'Ah, Melbourne, beautiful one day, dooms-day the next,' said Jack with a hearty laugh.

Will had to agree. From where he was sitting, the dark clouds rolling in did have that end-of-the-world look about them.

By the time the Victorian boys' side walked out to the oval to begin the match, the storm clouds were directly overhead.

The West Australian team, which had finished on top of Group B, won the toss and the captain chose to bat. It was a sensible choice considering the weather. Will watched the familiar face of Brock Anderson as he took up the crease at the striker's end.

'Hi, Willster!' Brock said cheerfully. 'Best of luck today.'

'Hey, Brock. Yeah . . . good luck to you guys too.'

Well, Brock certainly hadn't lost his polite nature since travelling back to Western Australia and taking up the opening spot for the Western Australian state team. Another thing he hadn't lost was his ability to smash the stuffing out of the ball. When Darren came steaming in and served up a scorching first ball, Brock simply leant back and timed a perfect late cut that took full advantage of Darren's pace and sent the ball hurtling towards the fence for four.

There's a guy who's not over-thinking things, mused Will at square leg. He was crouching down low, ready for a catch or run-out opportunity, but something told him it wouldn't happen while Brock was out in the middle.

Unfortunately for Victoria, Will was right. Brock and his opening partner weren't intimidated by Killer's speed. They went after the pace bowlers from the first over and managed to get Western Australia off to a blistering start. Brock seemed to know where every delivery was going to pitch before it had even left the bowler's hand, and he always seemed to have plenty of time to select a shot and move into position. After just six overs, Brock was on 45.

In no time at all Western Australia had cruised to 72 without loss. Mike decided enough was enough. He called Will over. 'Okay Will, we really need a wicket here. You have to break this partnership.'

'Okay,' said Will nervously.

'But, you know, no pressure,' added Mike.

'Right, no worries,' said Will. He took up the ball and headed to the northern end once again. Then something tapped him on the head.

Will looked up and a large fat raindrop splatted in his eye. Then another hit him in the face. A moment later, the clouds burst and the rain came down. And not just rain, there was thunder and lightning as well. The umpire signalled game off and the players jogged off the field while the groundsmen quickly dragged out the pitch covers. By the time the players got to the stand, the rain was pelting down.

'Maybe I won't need to take any wickets. Looks like the game will be a washout!' said Will hopefully as he and Mike took cover under the shelter of the grandstand.

'They can't call it off, it's a semifinal,' said Mike dourly. 'If the rain stops we'll still have to bat, and we'll need to better the Western Australian total by quite a bit, but in the same number of overs.'

'They're none for 72 from six! We'll never get more than that,' sighed Will.

'Better hope it doesn't stop raining then,' said Mike.

So Will closed his eyes and prayed for the rain to pour down. And it did. For 45 minutes. Then as quickly as it started, it stopped. The clouds broke and the blue sky reappeared and the umpires made the decision to use the Duckworth-Lewis method to calculate the score Victoria would need to win. Will had never been so disappointed to see the sun.

 # HIT AND RUN

'I know this seems like a big ask, boys,' said Jack as the groundsmen removed the covers and the umpires headed out to check the pitch. 'According to the Duckworth-Lewis method, we need 82 runs from six overs to win.' Jack gave a low whistle and clicked his tongue.

'But we've got two very good openers. They just need to go out there and play positive. If Western Australia can get the runs, then we can too!'

Jack finished by forcing a large smile and then nodded at Shavil and Riley. 'Well, go on, get out there, what are you waiting for?'

Shavil shot Will a tiny look of desperation. Will didn't know what to do. Finally he gave Shavil a determined fist pump in the air. Shavil limply pumped his fist back. The two smiled before Shavil and Riley walked out to face the first over of a near-impossible innings. Half an over later, it became a little nearer to impossible when Riley went searching for a cut shot and the ball struck the bottom edge of his bat, ricocheting onto the bails.

Jack looked over at Will, who reluctantly stood up and grabbed his bat, gloves and helmet. It took a moment for him to realise the whole team was looking at him.

They all think I'm going to blow it.

'Go get 'em, Will,' said Jack, with a steely resolve.

His teammates chimed in.

'Yeah, come on Will!'

'You've got this!'

They clapped him and patted his back as he made his way past them to the gate.

'Thanks guys,' said Will. At least his teammates were behind him.

When he got out in the middle Will turned to face the bowler. What had Maxi told him?

Watch the ball. Swing. Keep it simple . . .

The first ball suddenly zipped straight past him on the off side and Will had to contort his body to get his bat out of the way in time.

Stupid! I was too busy thinking about not thinking.

Just watch the ball, he told himself.

But the next ball was too good – right in the block hole.

There was no way for him to get that one to the boundary. None from five, chasing 82. They might as well just pack it in now.

Shavil signalled for Will to meet him in the middle. When he got there, Shavil looked at him with a tiny twinkle in his eyes.

'Stop trying to hit boundaries,' he whispered.

'What? But we need . . .' Will looked over at the scoreboard, '82 runs off five overs.'

'That's why they think you'll go for sixes not singles. They want you to take singles. Let's just play hit and run for a while.'

Will didn't understand Shavil's logic but when he faced the last ball of the over he did exactly what Shavil suggested and took an easy single. On the first ball of the next over, Will again found a single. The Western Australian players seemed happy with the result if it meant no boundaries. Shavil did the same from the second ball, putting Will back on strike. He looked around at the field placing. *Maybe I can grab a two if I get past mid-wicket.*

The third ball was also well placed, but Will managed to slot it perfectly between the mid-wicket fielder and the deep mid-on. He took off quickly and called 'two' to Shavil as they passed. The throw came low and fast as Will came back for the second but he glided the bat safely over the crease. Will couldn't believe his luck when the wickie fumbled the ball and it rolled away behind him. Will didn't have to say a word; Shavil was pounding down the pitch for the overthrow. Five runs off three. It was a start.

Shavil mistimed the next delivery but it struck the top of his pad and ran away right between the fielder at leg gully and the keeper. Four leg byes. Shavil took another single off the fifth and Will found himself back on strike for the last.

Ten runs off the over so far. They had done well. No need to get carried away.

Just watch the ball, Will told himself . . .

But when he saw the last delivery was pitched in short, his eyes lit up.

This time, he didn't need to think.

BANG!

Like a bullet from a gun, the ball screamed all the way to the fence. Six runs! That made it 16 off the over!

Just 66 runs to go, thought Will. *We can't do this . . . Can we?*

But two overs later, Will and Shavil were piling on the runs. They cut and drove and tapped and edged and took each and every run they could get. Sometimes it was one or two but more and more it was four or six. There were pretty shots, ugly shots, clever shots, not-so-clever shots, tiny strokes and massive slogs and each run brought down the total.

In the third they took nine and in the fourth they took 13. For the first time, the Western Australian players began to look nervous. When they set the field to stop the ones and twos, Will sent the ball flying into the air. When they put more fielders on the boundaries, Shavil would find a sneaky one or two.

In the fifth over, Will smashed two sixes in a row. Then he took a single, allowing Shavil to snatch three perfectly placed fours to bring it to 25 off the over. They had hit 63. They needed 19 off the last over.

'Give 'em singles, no boundaries,' called Brock desperately, and every man was pushed back to the fence.

'Fine with me,' said Will. He smacked the ball back into the gap at mid-on, but the fielder who ran in to collect it overran the ball. Will made a snap judgement and quickly called for another run. Shavil obliged and they raced off for another — just as the fielder recovered. He picked up the ball and threw it hard at the stumps. Will was well short of the crease and his heart leapt in his chest as he watched the ball head straight for the stumps . . .

MOMENT OF MIRTH

'Nooo!' cried the wickie.

The throw was wayward and missed the stumps by a metre.

The wickie had no chance of stopping it and the ball tore away along the outfield once more, leaving Will and Shavil time to take

another two runs before the ball was finally stopped just before the fence. They had four off the first ball of the over. Fifteen to go.

On the second ball, Will took to the air. But he'd miscued it. It went skyward and he watched as a fielder positioned himself directly under the ball.

'Run, Will!' screamed Shavil.

Will put his head down and ran. When he finally hazarded a look towards the fielder, he saw that the fielder had dropped it cold. Will couldn't believe his luck. First the near run-out and now a dropped catch! Shavil and Will somehow managed to come back for a second run and Will retained the strike.

Buoyed by his close escape, Will managed a pull shot off the third ball and they took another two runs. Now they needed 11 off three.

Will got hold of the fourth ball and this time it went all the way for six. He didn't hesitate in taking a single off the fifth ball — he knew if anyone could find the fence off the last ball it was Shavil.

The Western Australian players were freaking out. They took almost three minutes to place a field for the final ball.

But it didn't make any difference. Shavil timed the ball perfectly and it raced away to the boundary. Three players ran to stop it. The ball beat them all.

Will couldn't believe it. Shavil had done it. They had done it. They were through to the final.

The day before the final, the Victorian team met for a light training run on the academy oval. Most of the boys found it hard to focus: they were too busy thinking about the final showdown against New South Wales. Two teams would fight it out at the hallowed Melbourne Cricket Ground as the curtain raiser for the Big Bash match between the Melbourne Stars and the Sydney Sixers.

'I can't believe we're going to be playing at the MCG tomorrow night! My dad is so excited. He won't shut up about it,' said Will as he and Shavil ran through some paired fielding drills.

'I still can't believe we won,' said Shavil. 'I mean, what if I'd missed that last shot? We'd be watching Brock and his team play New South Wales.'

Will knew Shavil really had come through, winning the game on the final ball. Still, he couldn't help but tease his friend.

'Yeah, yeah, you saved the day. Can I have your autograph, Mr Kumar?'

'No, but you can shout me a blue slushie after training.'

'Who's shouting slushies?'

Will and Shavil turned to find Glenn Maxwell standing right behind them.

'Maxi!' shouted Shavil, unable to contain his excitement.

'Hi, Maxi,' said Will, trying hard to sound a little more subdued than Shavil.

'Hey, boys, great stuff yesterday – Jack told me all about it.'

Glenn was wearing his Melbourne Stars shirt and cap and looked almost ready to run out and play, which made Will curious. 'Are you here for training?'

'Actually,' explained Glenn, 'Jack invited some of the Melbourne Stars players along today to give you young guys a rev up – though after the way you two played yesterday, maybe you should be giving us the rev up.'

Will grinned. 'The advice you gave me the other day really helped. Though with only six overs, I didn't have too much time to over-think things anyway!'

Glenn winked at Will. 'Good to hear. Just remember to keep your eye on the ball and your mind clear tomorrow night.'

A moment later, a few of Glenn's team-mates arrived. Soon, Jack had them all playing a friendly game of hit and run. It wasn't long before the game became more serious, though. The Melbourne players may have been far more experienced, but that didn't stop them wanting to win against the boys. The boys were equally set on showing up the first-class players.

When Glenn had a bat, the boys were extra keen to take his wicket, but Maxi wasn't going to just give it away. He played plenty of his trademark shots, including two reverse sweep shots that had the boys running for miles. Finally, though, one of Glenn's shots went straight up in the air and Will ran as hard as he could to take a one-handed catch on the fly.

Will leapt up, beaming, with the ball still in his hand, and Glenn applauded him with his bat and his glove. When the training session was finished, Will still couldn't wipe the smile from his face and he felt a lot more excited than nervous about the final. He was feeling so good, he even shouted Shavil that blue slushie.

DOWN FOR THE COUNT

The first thing Will saw when he walked out through the players' entrance of the MCG was the Great Southern Stand. It towered over everything and made Will feel so small.

Will had been to the MCG to watch games with his dad before, but walking out from the tunnel and seeing the stadium from the ground was a completely different experience. He stopped for a moment. It was awe-inspiring and just a bit terrifying.

'What are you waiting for, Will? Get out there!' barked Darren from behind him. Will started walking again, but he couldn't stop his eyes from darting around the ground, trying their best to drink every detail. While the stands weren't even half-full yet – it was only 4.30 pm and the main game didn't start till eight – there were still a lot of spectators and more were streaming in. Some cheered and applauded as the boys took to the field. It was good to have the home-side advantage, thought Will, who was remembering the way New South

Wales had so thoroughly flogged them in the group match.

New South Wales had won the toss and, predictably, elected to bat. Jack had stressed how important it was for their team to bowl and field well. 'If they get a big score, we'll struggle to match it against their bowling line-up,' Jack had instructed as Dan Brockle-hurst ran the team through some last-minute warm-up stretches in the players' change room.

Now, as Will settled into his regular fielding position at short leg, he began to see that Jack was right. If New South Wales did post a big score, he wasn't sure his team could chase down the runs the way they had in the reduced overs match against Western Australia.

Will's fears were realised from the first over when the New South Wales openers made their intentions clear with four boundaries. Will watched poor Darren walk head down back to his fielding position. But while the second over from another country Victorian bowler, Joey Romeo, had also been savaged by the run-hungry New South Wales openers, when Darren returned to the northern end, he had a steely look that Will recognised from his own battles at the crease with Killer. He looked angry and determined.

Will got ready at short leg as Darren unleashed a monster of a bouncer. The New South Wales batsman tried to get out of the way but the ball bounced off his glove and into

'Lil' Benny Huynh's waiting hands behind the wicket. The team ran in and congratulated Darren, but he still had that angry determined look in his eyes. Three balls later, he took the wicket of the number-three batsman and the Victorians felt like they were getting on top.

But the feeling didn't last long.

Toby Gregg, the opener who had bashed the Victorian bowlers around so badly in their last encounter with New South Wales, was still out there doing damage. He skipped away to 42 off 19, despite Victoria's sharp fielding and Darren's killer bowling.

On the ninth over, Mike decided it was time to switch to their spin attack.

'Just keep it tidy; don't let them push you around,' advised Mike, looking at Will.

Will gave Mike a quick nod but a shudder rippled through him. He still had nightmarish visions of the mauling he'd received off his first over against New South Wales in the group game. Will tried to push the memory to the back of his mind. *No point thinking about that now. Just do what Maxi said . . . don't think.*

Will moved in and bowled his first delivery, focusing all his energy into getting the ball spinning, and throwing it a little higher for extra flight. It was a good ball, too. It turned a little and drifted through the air, bouncing high off the pitch and up into the batsman's face, which made it all the more frustrating when Toby Gregg stepped quickly onto the back foot and hooked it for six.

Will turned and walked back to his mark. He didn't want Toby Gregg to see his face. He didn't want anyone to see his face. He felt like it might shatter and fall into tiny pieces on the turf.

Not again! I can't let him smash me around again!

But no matter what he tried, each ball that Will bowled met with the same terrible fate; each was whacked with explosive force to the rope.

This time, Toby Gregg took 32 off Will's six balls and when the last was bowled, Will felt as if he were out on his feet, like a prize fighter down for the count.

After his one expensive over, Mike pulled Will from the attack. He didn't bowl again that night but that didn't stop the onslaught of runs. The New South Wales team was just getting started.

JUST KEEP SWINGING

Will sat, padded up, on the players' bench, and watched nervously as Shavil and Riley faced off against the intimidating New South Wales pace attack. They needed to score quickly: they were chasing 184 and, with a required run rate of over nine per over, they couldn't afford to take it easy.

Shavil started positively with a straight drive that gave him three runs and, soon after, a nicely guided edge that beat the slip fielders and raced away to the rope.

'Come on, Shavil!' called Will.

But the very next ball bounced up and found the fine edge of Shavil's bat – then flew straight through to the man at slips. The New South Wales players howled and the umpire raised his finger.

Will stood up slowly, unable to take his eyes off poor Shavil who was still looking back at the slips area trying desperately to somehow take back his loose shot. Finally, he tucked his bat under his arm and headed towards the pavilion.

'Bad luck, mate,' said Will when he passed Shavil.

'Stupid,' said Shavil, cursing himself. 'Guess you and Riley will have to save the day this time.'

Will gave Shavil a nod. He swung his bat through the air to loosen up his shoulders and jogged out to the middle of the MCG. This was what he had always dreamed of – playing at one of the best cricket grounds in the world – but all he could think about was the run chase. They were one for 12 in the third over. How were they going to get to 184?

The magic of their victory against Western Australia in the semifinal felt light-years away. Sure, they had been chasing a lot of runs, but Will only had to hit out for six overs. Now, if they were to win, he would have to stick around for a lot longer than that. They would need high scores for all 20 overs.

The first ball of the over came in fast and low and Will had to play it into the ground. Dot ball.

Just keep swinging, Will told himself.

The second ball was another yorker and Will bumped it back into the deck. Dot ball.

Patience, Will. Don't think about anything else.

Will watched the bowler run in.

Anticipate.

He won't bowl full again. He'll want to mix it up. Maybe drop it in short.

Act!

Will was right. The ball was pitched fast but short. He leapt onto the front foot and launched his bat at the ball. He could tell straightaway that it was going to be a six.

And it was. It was huge. It landed in the lower tier of the grandstand!

The crowd roared to life. They had come to watch the Melbourne Stars take on the Sydney Sixers but watching a local boy take it to a team from New South Wales was great pre-match entertainment.

Still, Will knew he had a long way to go.

Don't get too far ahead of yourself. Don't start thinking about it too much. Watch the ball. Anticipate. Act. One ball at a time.

So that's what he did. Will took on each ball, one at a time. He played each shot as if it were the only shot he had to hit. Sometimes he took a single, just like Shavil had told him to in the semifinal. Most times he managed to find the gaps in the field and, over by over, Will survived and the runs began to pile up.

The problem was that although Will was playing a steady game, his teammates were finding it more difficult. Riley went for 22 and there had been a steady flow of wickets for New South Wales ever since.

When Darren came out to bat, however, Will finally found a stable partner. Darren let Will do the heavy lifting but he kept the strike rotating with quick singles and the occasional boundary before starting to find the rope more often himself. Will couldn't believe that he and Darren were actually working well together as batting partners, but he stopped himself thinking too much about it and instead chose to trust the partnership.

After the fifteenth over, with Victoria sitting on a total of 120, Will and Darren met in the middle to talk tactics.

'We can do this,' said Will. 'We just need to lift the run rate a bit more. We still need 64, so if we can get up to 13 runs for the next five, we'll win it.'

'No problem,' said Darren.

And for two overs it wasn't a problem. The pair put on another 29 and all of sudden victory was in sight. But then Darren got a little too ambitious and tried to smash a six down the ground. Instead, he found the man in the outfield. Will lost his partner and they were eight down with 35 runs still to score. The crowd that had been increasingly vocal throughout the Victorian innings went deathly quiet and the shudder that had rippled through his body earlier now became a tidal wave of worry.

Just keep swinging, Will reminded himself.

PRIDE OF THE STATE

Will watched on as Joey Romeo jogged out to the centre of the MCG to take Darren's place. Joey was good with the ball but his strike rate with the bat was less impressive. Luckily he and Darren had crossed before he was caught so Will had the strike. Joey looked petrified.

I just need to hit twos, fours or sixes so I can stay on strike, decided Will, *then take a single off the last ball so I can face the next over as well. Simple.*

Of course, the New South Wales team was determined to get Joey on strike, so they made it as hard as possible for Will to hit out. For the next two deliveries, Will hit well-timed shots straight to fielders and had to send Joey back on both occasions. He didn't want the New South Wales bowler to have three consecutive balls at Joey. He reasoned that if they went nine wickets down it would make it so much harder, so he tried to be patient — but each dot ball was like a nail in the coffin. If the New South Wales bowlers got too many more, Victoria's chance of victory would be dead and buried.

Finally, on the fourth ball, Will got a good shot away. He took off like a rocket and turned for the second only to see Joey slip over at the crease. That moment's delay was all New South Wales needed. The return throw was low and hard and right on target at the batsman's end. Will and Joey had missed their chance for a second run. Joey would have to see out the over.

Will signalled for Joey to block. Joey nodded but when the New South Wales bowler steamed in and delivered a nasty bouncer, Joey put his body on the line and the ball struck him hard on the elbow. The keeper missed the ball and it rolled away to the fence. Four leg byes. They were down to 30. Will clapped Joey, who smiled awkwardly while rubbing his elbow.

Unfortunately for Joey, the bouncer was just the entree. The next ball was the main course and it ripped through middle stump like a hurricane. Will closed his eyes as the opposition's cheers of jubilation filled his ears. They had one wicket left: Kurt Mallia, who was even less confident with a bat than Joey was. And they still needed 30 runs with 12 balls in hand.

It's not going to happen, whispered a dark voice at the back of Will's head. Will tried to shake it away. *Don't think about it!*

The only good news was that Will was on strike. The bad news was he could no longer afford to be choosey about scoring opportunities. He would have to take any runs on offer.

But the new New South Wales bowler wasn't offering any. They had brought back their spinner for this second-last over and his slow-placed turn was devilishly hard to score off. For the first three balls, Will failed to get a shot away. He looked around the ground but all the gaps he had been so good at spotting throughout the match seemed to have disappeared. Frustrated, he punched a drive through to mid-on and hoped there would be a misfield or an overthrow. There wasn't. Kurt was on strike.

Will didn't want to watch, but he had to be ready if Kurt somehow got a single away. Kurt missed the next ball completely and it drifted perilously close to leg stump. Then on the last ball of the over, the second-worst thing that could have happened did. The spinner bowled a wide. He would have to bowl one more. Will and Kurt both dropped their heads simultaneously. One more ball. Will signalled to Kurt to block.

The last ball was dead on target and Kurt did his best to get his bat in the way but the ball struck the top of his pad.

'Howzat!' screamed the bowler, as the whole New South Wales team roared in appeal for LBW. Will looked to the umpire. The umpire cocked his head to the side, as if considering what to do, and Will felt his heart leap in his chest.

Slowly the umpire shook his head. Kurt had survived and Will was on strike.

One more over to score 28 runs. Will's heart sank. It seemed impossible.

'Too bad you're not bowling against yourself, then you might have had a chance!' sang a merry voice from the slips, followed by a chorus of laughs.

Will turned and saw the beaming smile of Toby Gregg, the New South Wales captain who had scored 32 off Will's one over. He smirked contentedly at Will and Will had no answer but to look away.

Then something occurred to him.

If he can do it, why can't I? Surely I'm not that bad a bowler — and he got 32. Twenty-eight runs in an over isn't as hard as 32. I can do it. I just need to swing at every ball and hope for the best.

Determined, Will faced his first ball of the final over. It was a yorker, but Will bounced back on his toes and scooped the ball skyward.

It went up and up and up. The New South Welshman in the outfield went back for it. It looked like he would take it easily but right as he got his hands to it, his momentum took him over the rope. Six runs.

The crowd, which had been quiet for the last few overs, roared back to life. It was as if Will's six had jump-started their hearts.

Twenty-two from five, Will thought. *I can do it.*

The next ball was low and wide but Will wasn't going to let that stop him. He swung his bat hard and caught the ball with the toe. It ran away through the off side, beat two fielders and bounced away for four.

The crowd screamed. Will imagined that somewhere in all that noise were the cheers of his mum and dad, all his teammates and Jack – and maybe Zoe, too.

Eighteen from four.

The next ball was wide of off stump again so Will just pretended he was Maxi. He dropped to one knee and reverse swept the ball with all his might. He'd been hoping for at least four. It went for six.

Toby Gregg and the bowler furiously talked tactics. The roar of the crowd was deafening, but Will's mind was on the team. He didn't want to let them down now. They were so close.

Twelve from three.

The bowler avoided the off side and jabbed it in down the middle, short and hard, hoping the bouncer would throw Will. And it almost

did. Will stuck his head down and swung his bat wildly at the ball. It disappeared into the twilight sky and no one knew where it went until it plummeted back to earth, landing a few metres beyond the rope.

The bowler shook his head and Toby ran in again to counsel him. Will took the time to scan the ground again. The entire crowd was on its feet.

Six from two. I can do it.

Will turned and watched the bowler sprint in. He saw the bowler's hand roll over and release the ball. He watched as the ball came hurtling towards him like a miniature meteor.

Anticipate.

Yorker. He wants to jam me.

Act!

Will leapt to the front foot before the ball had reached him and swung through the line of the ball.

And just like the third ball he had faced, Will knew as soon as he had struck it that it was going all the way for six.

They had won! And with one ball to spare!

All of a sudden, nothing seemed real. It was as if Will's mind had left his body and was floating up above the stadium. The crowd erupted but the cheers seemed far away. Out of the corner of his eye, he saw Kurt Mallia running towards him and before he knew it, they were hugging and dancing on the pitch.

Will turned back towards the wicket and saw a familiar face in front of him. It was

Toby Gregg, his face white with disbelief. Will walked right over and shook his hand.

'Good game,' he said. Toby nodded but his miserable face became a lot more miserable.

Will and Kurt trotted triumphantly back to the pavilion where the whole team was waiting in a guard of honour. Will was being bombarded with back slaps and hair ruffles when he saw Zoe.

'Willster, that was amazing! I'm so proud of you,' Zoe yelled over the noise of the crowd. Before Will knew it she had planted a kiss on his cheek.

Will was stunned. But even more stunning was the TV camera crew and sports reporter who had appeared in front of him.

'I'm standing here with young Will Albright who, after pulling off a stunning

VICTORIA 2ND INNINGS		RUNS	BF	FOW
KUMAR, S	c. GREGG b. ROGERS	7	7	12
BRENNAN, R	c. XAVIER b. PARKER	22	16	43
ALBRIGHT, W	**NOT OUT**	**85***	**42**	
BRIGGS, R	b. GRAINGER	8	8	51
SANNA, A	c. GRAINGER b. GRAINGER	4	5	58
HUYNH, B	st. BAXTER b. BANNER	1	4	60
REYNOLDS, M	c. RICHARDS b. ROGERS	18	11	96
ZAMMIT, A	c. POTTER b. GRAINGER	0	1	96
McKINNON, D	c. BAXTER b. ROGERS	32	22	149
ROMEO, J	b. PARKER	0	2	154
MALLIA, K	**NOT OUT**	**0***	**3**	
EXTRAS (2w, 1nb, 4lb)		7		

VIC: 9/184 TARGET: 184
RUNS REQ: 0   **VICTORIA WINS!**
BALLS REMAINING: 1

NSW	O	M	R	W	ER
ROGERS, S	4	0	38	3	9.50
PARKER, P	3.5	0	53	2	15.14
GRAINGER, J	4	0	34	3	8.50
BANNER, D	4	0	26	1	6.50
STARK, T	4	0	31	0	7.75

NSW 1ST INNINGS: 183   OVER: 19.5   THIS OVER: 6 4 6 6 6

victory in the final of the T20 National Youth Shield, is about to become the most talked-about youngster in Victoria. Will, how does it feel to win like that in front of a home crowd?'

Will thought for a moment and then looked at the camera. 'Unreal!' he said finally.

'And where to now, Will?' asked the reporter.

'I'm hoping someone's going to shout me and my team slushies!' said Will.

The reporter gave Will a strange look but he could tell that Shavil, who was standing close by, knew exactly what Will was talking about. Shavil smiled at Will. It didn't get any better than this.

GLENN MAXWELL

Nicknames: Maxi

Born: 14 October 1988 in Kew, Victoria

Height: 182 cm

Weight: 74 kg

Batting style: Right-hand bat

Bowling style: Right-arm orthodox

Role: All-rounder

National side: Australia

MAXI'S TOP T20 TIPS FOR OVERCOMING A FORM SLUMP AND CHASING —— DOWN A TOTAL ——

Overcoming a form slump

Whether you're a professional cricketer, a club cricketer or just a casual player, anyone can go through a form slump from time to time. Usually these slumps are psychological rather than physical, although when you're not scoring runs and your confidence is down, your technique can suffer as well. Here are a few tips to help you overcome that slump and start scoring runs again.

- **Avoid over-analysing why you are out of form.** Don't over-think things. Over-focusing on a lack of runs can distract you from getting the little things right.

- **Practise.** At training, have your coach or a friend watch you bat in the net to make sure you are still using good technique and have your head, hands and feet in the right position. Facing balls in the nets will help with your confidence come match day.

- **Take things slowly.** When you're playing a match, try to stay relaxed and don't be in a rush to score runs. Be conservative and avoid risky shots. Look for singles to keep the strike rotating so that you can take some of the pressure off yourself. The more time you spend in the middle, the more likely you will be to find your form.

- **Watch the ball.** Often this one simple thing can be forgotten when you're feeling pressure to perform. Make sure you watch the ball as it moves all the way from the bowler's hand to the bat. You can't hit what you don't see.

Doing the simple things well and clearing your mind of negative thoughts about performing badly will help you find your way back to winning form.

Chasing down a total

There's no doubt that in all forms of cricket, chasing down a total is a vital skill, but in T20 games the run chase has almost become an art form. Handling the pressure at the pointy end of the game is no easy feat; it takes the right measure of confidence, caution and timing. Here are a few things to keep in mind.

- **Believe in yourself.** There's not much point trying to chase down a total that you don't think you can get. Start with the mindset that you will win the match.

- **Make a plan.** Once you've begun to believe you will win the match, start thinking about a plan for how you will do it. Have an idea about how much you need to score off each over and look for chances to play aggressively and find the boundary. Be strategic about when you hit out and against which bowlers. Breaking the total down into chunks of ten or 20 runs can also help you feel more confident about chasing down a big total. Each time you secure another chunk of the total, you will feel closer to the win.

- **Intend to score.** Having the intention to score is vital when you're chasing runs. Play your shots but remember you can't hit boundaries off every ball. Rotate the strike to avoid one player getting bogged down at one end.

- **Take it one ball at a time.** When it comes to chasing runs, you need to play each ball as it comes. There may be times when you need to adjust your plan, such as after the loss of a wicket or an over from a great bowler. Don't panic or resort to rash shots. Have faith that there will be more scoring opportunities to come.

With the right mindset and focus you can recover from any setback and find a way to chase down that total.

GLOSSARY

all-rounder   a player who bowls, bats and fields equally well

arm ball   a delivery from a slow bowler which has no spin on it, thus producing an unexpected straight-on flight

beamer   a full toss, usually fast, which goes towards the head of the person batting; an illegal delivery, punishable by a no ball being called

block hole   the area between the batsman's bat and toes

bosie   see *googly*

bouncer   a ball which is so bowled that it bounces high when it pitches; also known as a bumper

boundary
a) the marked limits of the field
b) the score of four derived from hitting a ball which reaches the boundary
c) the score of six derived from hitting a ball which goes over the boundary before it touches the ground

bumper	see *bouncer*
bye	a run made on a ball not struck by the person batting
captain's knock	a batting innings by the captain of a team of such quality that befits his or her position, especially one that is a turning point in the game
carrom ball	similar to a doosra except that the ball is spun using the thumb and the middle finger
caught-and-bowled	a dismissal in which the bowler takes the catch
century	100 runs
clean-bowl	to break the wicket without touching the person batting or their bat
cover drive	a drive which sends the ball towards or past cover point (a fielding position between point and mid-off)
crease	one of three lines marked near each wicket: i) bowling crease, along which the stumps are placed ii) popping crease, behind which some part of the bowler's front foot must land when bowling iii) return crease, marking the limits for the bowler at each side of the popping crease

cross-bat   a bat moving in a horizontal curve, as for a cut shot

cut shot   a) in batting, to strike with a cross-bat and dispatch a ball on the off side, usually in a direction between cover and third man
b) in bowling, to cause the ball to deviate on bouncing, usually by making the seam strike the pitch

declare   to close an innings voluntarily before all 10 wickets have fallen

delivery   the act of bowling a ball

doosra   an off-spinner's googly, which looks similar to a normal off-break, but rather than spinning towards the bat, goes the other way, in the manner of a leg break

dot ball   a delivery from which no runs are scored

drop   a falling wicket

Duckworth-Lewis method   a mathematical formula used to calculate the target number of runs for the team batting second in a limited-overs cricket match that has been interrupted

fast bowling   a style of bowling in which the ball is delivered at high speeds; also known as pace bowling

finger spinner a bowler who uses an action of the fingers to impart spin

googly a delivery bowled by a wrist spinner which looks as if it will break one way but in fact goes the other; also known as a bosie or wrong 'un

half-century an individual score of over 50 runs, but not over 100 runs

half-volley a delivered ball or its return, hit or kicked the moment after it bounces from the ground

helicopter shot a stroke played by swinging the bat in an uppercut fashion so that it catches the ball partly from below; in the follow-through the bat flails up and around vertically, through an angle that may exceed 180 degrees

innings
a) the turn of one member of the batting team to bat
b) one of the major divisions of a match, consisting of the turns at batting of all the members of one team until they are all out or until the team declares
c) the runs scored during such a turn or such a division

inswing the movement from off to leg of a bowled ball

LBW (leg before wicket)	a dismissal that occurs if the ball, when pitching in line with the stumps, strikes the batsman's leg or pads and so is impeded from hitting the wicket
leg break	a ball which, when a right-hander is facing, changes direction from leg to off when it pitches
leg glance	a glancing stroke by the person batting directing the ball down fine on the leg side of the wicket
leg side	that half of the field which is behind the person batting who is facing the bowling, as opposed to off side
leg spin	the spin which a bowler imparts to a ball to achieve a leg break
long-off	an off side fielding position behind the bowler, or a fielder in this position
medium-pace	a style of bowling which is slower than pace bowling but faster than spin bowling
mid-off	a fielding position on the off side, near the bowler
mid-on	a fielding position on the on side near the bowler
no ball	a ball bowled in a way disallowed by the rules and automatically giving the side batting a score of one run counted as a sundry

non-striker	the batsman standing at the bowling end
off-break	a ball which, when a right-hander is facing, changes direction from off towards leg when it pitches
off-cutter	a delivery from a fast bowler, similar to an off-break, but at greater speed
off side	the half of the field towards which the feet of the person batting point as he or she stands ready to receive the bowling, as opposed to leg side
off-spin	the spin which a bowler imparts on a ball to achieve an off-break
off stump	the stump on the off side of the person batting
on side	see *leg side*
opener	either of the two people batting who open their side's innings by batting first
outfield	the part of the field furthest from the person batting
outswing	the movement from leg to off of a bowled ball
over	a) the number of balls delivered between successive changes of bowlers b) the part of the game played between such changes

overpitch	to bowl so that the ball bounces too far up the wicket, allowing the person batting to play it with ease
pace bowling	a style of bowling in which the ball is delivered at high speeds; also known as fast bowling
pitch	a) to bowl so that the ball bounces on a certain part of the wicket b) when a ball bounces on a certain part of the wicket
plumb	a batter standing directly in front of the wicket and thus leg before wicket or potentially leg before wicket
pull	to hit (a ball pitched on the wicket or on the off side) to the on side, usually off the back foot
reverse sweep	a shot in which the batter drops to one knee and reverses the hands in gripping the bat so as to sweep the ball from leg to off
run-out	the dismissal of the person batting by being run out
run rate	the number of runs scored per over, assessed by dividing the score by the number of overs completed
short-pitched	of or relating to a bowled ball which first strikes the pitch at a short distance from the bowler

slider   a delivery from a spin bowler that involves placing back spin on the ball so it often skids or slides off the pitch

slip fielder   a close fielder behind the batsman, next to the wicketkeeper

slog sweep   a pull shot that is played from kneeling position, usually against full-pitched, slower balls, in an attempt to hit boundaries

spin bowler   a bowler who has a special skill in spinning the ball

square leg   a fielding position on the leg side at right angles to the pitch opposite the wicket of the person batting

straight drive   a batted shot that passes straight past the bowler

sundry   a score or run not made by hitting the ball with the bat, as a bye or a side; an extra

sweep   to strike the ball with a cross-bat close to the ground, on the leg side, usually backward of square leg

switch hit   a shot played by a batsman who reverses both their stance and their grip during the bowler's run-up so that a right-handed batsman would play the shot as an orthodox left-hander

tailenders   a team member who is ranked towards the end in the batting order

topspinner   a delivery in which forward spin is imparted to the ball, so that it does not deviate significantly on bouncing, but accelerates off the pitch, and often bounces unexpectedly high

wicketkeeper   the player on the fielding side who stands immediately behind the wicket to stop balls that pass it; also known as a wickie

wrist spinner   a bowler who uses an action of the wrist to impart spin

wrong 'un   see *googly*

yorker   a ball so bowled that it pitches directly under the bat

Watch out for the fourth

Glenn Maxwell book

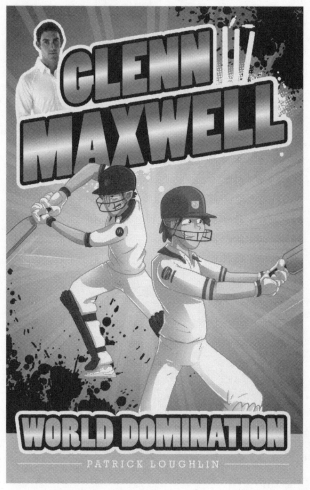

OUT NOW

Have you missed the first two

Glenn Maxwell books?

OUT NOW

OUT NOW